# Sleep Stories for Kids:
# Jinx the Cat

Fulton Smith

# Table of Contents

# Chapter 1:

# Jinx's Family

Jinx the Cat is in many ways a typical black cat. He's smart-like most cats are-especially black cats. He's beautiful, too, with smooth black fur that shines like moonlight on a dark sea as he walks around his home. But Jinx is unique, too! You might have already guessed his special feature from his name: Jinx. That's right; Jinx is unfortunately blessed with more than a little bad luck. Sometimes it happens to him, and sometimes it happens to whoever is nearby at the wrong time.

Jinx lives with his family of humans in a neat little town house. There are three humans in his family: Dad, Mom, and a little human girl named Sally. One day, when Jinx had just come to his home, Dad got out a big scary machine that made an awful noise. It was roaring as Dad pushed it across the carpet. Jinx immediately jumped up and hid on top of the refrigerator, but then as he peeked his little black head over the side of the fridge, he saw it roaring towards Sally's room. Poor Sally wouldn't stand a chance against that monster!

Jinx wasn't sure what to do, but finally, he made his choice. Remembering all the nice scratches, treats, and play times he had had with Sally, he lept into action. Landing gracefully on all four paws, Jinx sprinted to the door of Sally's room just in time, arched his back, and hissed his meanest hiss at that awful machine. It stopped roaring immediately, and backed away, obviously frightened by Jinx. Then, Jinx saw Dad laughing.

"It's only the vacuum cleaner, Jinx," he explained kindly. Then, he petted Jinx's ears, picked him up, and gave him to Sally, who was also laughing in the doorway. Sally took Jinx to play in another room. Mom cleaned up the vase and flowers that Jinx had knocked off the refrigerator.

Jinx learned many new things about his home, like how the scary vacuum cleaner actually wasn't dangerous at all. He also learned how to get water from the taps. Whenever he was thirsty, he would meow at his water bowl until a human came to give him water, but every time they did, they would sigh, scold him, and say, "Jinx! Your water bowl is already full of water!" Jinx didn't like to be scolded by his humans, though he always pretended not to notice at all. Jinx didn't like stale water either, though, so he would always meow for fresh water when he was thirsty.

Then, Jinx had an idea. After he meowed for his water as usual, he watched carefully as Mom took his water bowl to the sink, emptied it, and then turned the tap to refill it. Jinx saw from where the cool, fresh water was coming. So, after Mom put his water bowl down, Jinx jumped up on the counter, pushed the tap with his nose until the fresh water came out, and then lapped it up happily. No more needing to meow and wait for it!

# Chapter 2:

# Jinx Explores the Neighborhood

One day, Jinx was bored. He had learned everything there was to learn about his home. He knew how to get his own water. He knew just where to lie so the sun would warm him when he napped in the morning, and where to lie so the sun would warm him when he napped in the afternoon. He knew all of Sally's games, and he knew when Dad would sit on the easy chair, so he could lay in his lap and be nice and warm while he napped in the evening.

It was time for Jinx to see what was outside

the house. The problem was that the windows all had screens, and Jinx couldn't open the outside door. So, he stood at the door and meowed. Eventually, Mom came by and frowned.

"I don't think it's a good idea for you to go outside, Jinx," said Mom.

"Meow," answered Jinx. That was almost all Jinx knew how to say. 'Hiss' or 'purr' weren't right, so 'meow' would have to do. Jinx also put his paws on the door to get the message across.

Mom sighed and said, "I guess we'll have to try getting you a harness. Then you can go outside to play safely." Then, Mom walked away from the door.

Jinx didn't know what Mom meant, but no matter how he meowed and scratched at the door,

Mom wouldn't open it for him. Never mind. By now, Jinx knew that Sally would be coming home soon. So, Jinx waited by the door patiently.

It felt like it took forever, but finally Jinx woke up from his nap with his ears twitching at the sound of Sally walking towards the door from the outside. He instantly crouched into action, bottom in the air, ready to spring out, and when the door opened, Jinx was off like a shot into the great outdoors!

The very first thing Jinx noticed as soon as he was outside was how bright the sun was! Jinx blinked his eyes and immediately ran into the shadow of the bushes right against the front of the house. The second thing Jinx noticed was the sound of Sally crying out for him to come back. Jinx wanted to tell Sally he would come back soon, but all he could say was 'meow' or 'purr' or 'hiss', and none of those seemed right, so Jinx just pushed back further into the bushes as Sally came after him.

Eventually, Jinx pushed right through the other side. Then he burst out into the bright sunlight again, turned tail, and ran towards the street. He immediately saw several gigantic, metal machines roaring down the street towards him from both directions. He flattened his ears back, sprinted across as fast as he could, and climbed right up a nearby tree. Far below, he saw Sally looking for him, but he was safe where he was for now.

After a few moments high up in the tree, Jinx

calmed down and felt safe again. He took in all the sights of the outside world. Birds flew around cheeping and cawing, and Jinx felt he could almost reach out and paw one, but none ever came close enough to him. He saw little bugs climbing on the tree branches and more strange humans than he could imagine walking around and even sitting inside the huge metal machines. He climbed down the tree slowly, hopped onto a fence post, and walked along the top of it gingerly.

After a short walk past a few town houses, his ears twitched. He heard something coming from an alleyway behind the house he had just passed. He turned back to follow the sound. It was very faint, but as he got closer, Jinx could hear it more clearly. Then he picked up the scent, too. It was like him, but different. Jinx couldn't wait to see what it was. But then he smelled something different... something dangerous. Jinx continued the approach more cautiously.

# Chapter 3:

# Jinx's Amazing Discovery

Jinx walked along the fence top carefully, towards the sound that had him so curious. As he came to the edge, where it disappeared around the corner of a housing duplex, he stopped and carefully peaked his head around the corner to see what he could hear and smell.

Across the alleyway was an overturned cardboard box, and looking out of that box was a tiny, lone kitten, meowing desperately. Looking into the box was something Jinx had seen before through windows, but never encountered face to face: a big, yellow dog! It was only inches from the poor defenseless kitten. Jinx knew he had to act in an instant.

With a courageous yowl, Jinx launched himself off the fence towards that big, yellow dog. The poor dog was taken completely by surprise! With a yelp, it jumped up and away from Jinx at the last instant, and Jinx crashed into the cardboard box at top speed. Jinx panicked as the box flipped over and everything went dark. He frantically darted around trying to get out before he remembered the poor kitten, who had been frightened into silence by the commotion.

When Jinx got his wits back, his eyes adjusted to the darkness, and he could see a flap that he could push to get out of the box. He could also feel something around his neck. That was strange! Normally Jinx hated things on his body, but this thing felt somehow kind of nice. Jinx checked on the kitten, and when he touched his nose to the kitten, he heard the kitten speak.

"Who are you?"

"What?" Jinx asked in surprise. He had heard people speaking before, and heard animal sounds, but he had never known exactly what any of it meant. He could only guess. But this was clear as his own voice in his head.

"I said, who are you?" repeated the bewildered kitten.

"Oh, uhh, I'm Jinx," said Jinx after a moment's thought. Then, "I'm here to rescue you from that nasty, big dog!" he bravely added.

"Oh," said the kitten, "But I like that dog. She's friendly. She brings me treats sometimes."

"What? Really?" Jinx asked, shocked. He cautiously poked his nose out of the box. Staring back at him through the opening was the big, yellow dog, now significantly more brown after being unluckily scared into a muddy puddle by Jinx's surprise attack. As Jinx's eyes adjusted to the bright light of the sun, the dog's nose touched him.

"Hey, what's the big idea!?" asked the dog, "You'll hurt that poor kitten! And you scared me half to death!"

"Um, sorry about that," replied Jinx sheepishly. "I thought I was saving that kitten from you."

"Haha, saving the kitten from me?" barked the

dog. "I was just giving her some treats! Say, wait a minute; how can you understand me so well? How can I understand you?" The dog backed up a few steps with a confused look on her face.

"Well, I don't know," said Jinx. "I've never been able to understand anyone else so well before either...." Jinx then took a few steps outside of the box.

"Well, that's a mighty nice collar you've got there!" said the dog approvingly. Jinx touched his neck with a paw and felt he was indeed wearing a collar. It must have slipped onto his head while he was tumbling through the box.

"Oh, really?" asked Jinx, unsure of what else to say. "Well, thank you, I guess." Jinx didn't want to sound any more foolish than he already felt, so he pretended the collar had always been there. "My name is Jinx; what's yours?"

"Well, my master calls me 'Bella'. Nice to meet you," she answered.

"Your master?" asked Jinx, not sure what Bella meant.

"Oh, here he comes now," said Bella. And sure enough, walking towards them was a big, human man with a friendly looking smile.

"Bella, there you are! What have you found now?" the man asked as he walked up to them.

Jinx disappeared back inside the box, then came out, gently holding the kitten by the scruff of her neck. Jinx wasn't sure why, but he felt he could trust the big friendly dog and her big friendly-looking human.

"Aww, look at the little kitty," said the man as he squatted down. "Are you the mommy cat?" he asked Jinx, as he reached out towards him. Jinx instinctively ducked back from his hand, though, and dropped the kitten as he backed away.

The man frowned as he considered the situation.

"Hmm, no," he was thinking out loud, "You look a little too young and thin to be this baby's mommy, and you're obviously not nursing. And you have a beautiful collar, while this poor kitten has been abandoned. That wouldn't make any sense. You must have your own home and just found this kitten the same time as Bella."

Bella nodded and wagged her tail enthusiastically, and the man patted her head affectionately.

The man picked up the kitten and checked her over carefully.

"What's he doing?" mewed the kitten.

"Don't worry; I think this man will help you," answered Jinx. Sure enough, the man gathered up the kitten in his arms, along with a little rag of a blanket in the box, and began walking carefully home with Bella following right at his heels.

Jinx thought it was about time for him to get back home, too. So, he jumped back up on the fence, followed his scent to the tree he had climbed, and then back across the road to his own home. Sally was still there, calling for him fearfully. Jinx calmly walked up to her as if nothing at all was amiss, and Sally instantly dropped down to gather him up in her arms.

"Jinx, where have you been!?" asked Sally, half angrily and half in relief.

"Oh, just down the street, Sally. Relax, I'm fine!"

Sally dropped right down on her bottom, and her jaw dropped straight down to her chest.

"Did... did you just talk to me?" asked Sally in amazement.

"Oh, you can hear me, too?" answered Jinx.

"... Mom! Dad! You won't believe this!" called Sally into the house.

# Epilogue

What will Sally's parent's think? Will Jinx meet Bella and the little kitten again? What adventures will Jinx go on next? Read the next stories to find out! And if you liked this story, please leave a review!